The Untold Story of Cinderella

RUSSELL SHORTO

Illustrated By T. Lewis

Here is Cinderella's sister's version of this famous story

Turn the book over and read the story from Cinderella's point of view

A Citadel Press Book

Published by Carol Publishing Group

First Carol Publishing Group Edition 1992

A Citadel Press Book
Published by Carol Publishing Group
Citadel Press is a registered trademark of Carol Communications, Inc.

Editorial Offices : 600 Madison Avenue, New York, NY 10022
Sales & Distribution Offices: 120 Enterprise Avenue, Secaucus, NJ 07094
In Canada: Canadian Manda Group, P.O. Box 920, Station U, Toronto,
Ontario, M8Z 5P9, Canada

Queries regarding rights and permissions should be addressed to Carol
Publishing Group, 600 Madison Avenue, New York, NY 10022

Manufactured in the United States of America
ISBN 0-8065-1298-9

10 9 8 7 6 5 4 3 2 1

Carol Publishing Group books are available at special discounts
for bulk purchases, for sales promotions, fund raising, or
educational purposes. Special editions can also be created to
specifications. For details contact: Special Sales Department,
Carol Publishing Group, 120 Enterprise Ave., Secaucus, NJ 07094

Library of Congress Cataloging-in-Publication Data

Shorto, Russell.
      Cinderella and Cinderella's stepsister / Russell Shorto;
illustrated by T. Lewis.
          p.   cm.

          Summary: After reading the classic tale of Cinderella, the reader
is invited to turn the book upside down and read an updated version
told from the "evil" stepsister's vantage point.
              1. Toy and movable books--Specimens. [1. Fairy tales.
2. Folklore. 3. Toy and movable books.] I. Lewis, T. (Thomas),
ill. II. Title. III. Title: Cinderella's stepsister.
PZ8.S344C1   1990
[398.2]--dc20
                                                                        90-41900
                                                                           CIP
                                                                           AC

I'm sure you know the story of Cinderella,
the poor girl with the wicked stepsisters who ended up
marrying a prince. But I'll bet you haven't heard the
real story. That's because Cinderella changed it a good
bit. Now, Cinderella was pretty and smart, but she had
one very bad habit. She liked to make up stories.

My name is Dora. I am one of Cinderella's stepsisters. But I am not at all wicked. And neither is my sister, Della. And our mother Donna, is one of the sweetest and kindest people in the world! In fact, she used to knit warm clothes for the poor and feed lost dogs and cats. But Cinderella really gave us all a bad reputation with her fantastic stories.

Cinderella was always in trouble for telling stories. Her father made her stand in the corner by the fireplace for punishment. She stood there so often, getting cinders in her hair, that one day she cried, "You might as well call me Cinderella!" That's how she *really* got her name.

Then came the day of the prince's ball. Cinderella made up quite a story for that. "I am just a poor girl with tattered clothes," she sighed. "But my Fairy Godmother will use magic and give me what I need to go to the ball."

Now, this was ridiculous. Cinderella's father was always giving her nice clothes—clothes which she never took care of.

That evening, Cinderella came out of her room wearing a beautiful silver-blue gown and a pair of tiny slippers that were so glittery they might have been made of glass.

"Look!" she exclaimed. "My Fairy Godmother has visited me. She has turned my tattered rags into beautiful clothes!"

And, with that, Cinderella glided outside. She stepped into the coach my stepfather had hired for us, and commanded the coachmen to drive on. Della and I had to walk to the palace. Luckily it wasn't far.

At the ball, we saw Cinderella looking around for the prince. None of us had ever seen him. Then she spotted him in the middle of the dance floor. He was a bit plump to be considered "dashing." Nevertheless, there could be no doubt that he was the prince, since everyone was crowded around him, laughing and hanging on his every word.

When the dance music began, Cinderella boldly

marched right up to the prince and cooed, "Thank you, your highness, I am honored!" As they danced, she told him all about herself—only, of course, it was all made up. "I am a princess from a faraway kingdom," she told him. "In fact, my kingdom is in the clouds. I came to earth on a magical moonbeam . . . just to dance with you, prince."

"How wonderful!" the prince exclaimed. Then he

told her all about himself. It was a thrilling story of palaces and riches and slaying dragons and other royal conquests. Cinderella was quite swept off her feet.

Cinderella was having a wonderful time. But then the clock began to chime twelve. Her father had declared that she must be home by twelve o'clock sharp, or else he would take away all her privileges. He was as tired of her coming home late as he was of her stories.

Cinderella slipped out of the prince's arms. "Oh, I must go!" she cried. "If I am not back in my cloud palace by midnight, the magical moonbeam will fade and I will be trapped on earth! Goodnight, dear prince!"

She flew down the palace steps, losing her shoe in her haste. But did she go back to get it? No, indeed—which shows you how well she took care of her things.

When Cinderella arrived home late, her father was angry. "But Papa," she began sweetly, "the carriage was attacked by bandits. The bandits turned into wolves, and they wanted to eat me. Then . . .

"Enough!" her father shouted. "No more of your silly stories! You are a bad girl, and you must be punished. You must stay in your room for one whole month! And no more clothes for two months!"

Cinderella went to her room and cried all night. She was still crying the next morning, when she heard a horseman outside her window. It was the prince. He had traced her here by means of her lost slipper.

He rushed into her room and immediately asked her to marry him. Cinderella realized that this was the moment to tell the truth.

"I'm afraid I am not a princess of the clouds," she told him sadly. "I live here with my father, my stepmother, and two stepsisters. I am only a girl who likes to tell stories. I don't suppose you want to marry me anymore."

"Nonsense!" he declared. "We'll be married on Saturday—that is, if you'll still have me. I too have a confession. I am not the prince at all, but only his second cousin. You mistook me for the prince at the ball, and I couldn't help but pretend. You see, I also have a habit of making up stories."

And so Cinderella and the prince's second cousin were married, and they made a perfect couple. They moved into a little cottage, which they called Castle of the Air, and they passed the time telling each other amazing stories. People said they had such a talent they should go into the fairy tale business. So that's just what they did. Together they made up all sorts of wonderful fairy tales, and told them to the children of the kingdom. They became the greatest storytellers of the day.

And every story they told ended with these words: ". . . and everyone lived—happily—ever—after!"

The End

ABOUT THE AUTHOR

Cheryl DeVleeschouwer is a first-time writer, but long-time fan of reading, stories, and literature. Originally written in 1990, Cheryl drafted *Elfie the Elf* for a graduate class. Her own kids loved the book so much that she often read it to them at night. Now almost 30 year later, *Elfie the Elf* has been officially published and illustrated so that families across the world can enjoy the holiday spirit and magic of Elfie.

Cheryl lives in New Jersey with her husband Rick and dog Charlie. While her children have now grown into adults, Cheryl still enjoys coming up with new stories for her two grandsons!

"Granny, do you still have the tape? We want to hear the song," Rosy and James begged.

"Alright! If you both go to bed right now, I'll hunt for the tape first thing in the morning and we'll listen to Elfie the Elf."

Rosy and James snuggled up in their beds and fell fast asleep hoping morning would be just a blink away.

"But how did you get home?" Rosy asked.

"I don't remember. I guess Santa took me home," Granny proudly spoke.

"Did you ever go back and visit Elfie and Santa Claus?" questioned James.

"That's the funny thing. As many times as I tried, I never could find my way back to Santa Land. All I remember is finding a letter and a tape inside my Christmas stocking the next morning. In fact, I think that letter is hiding somewhere in my pocket."

Granny pulled the crumpled, tattered piece of paper from her pocket and began reading.

"Dear Jessica, Thank you for all your help. The other elves and I will never forget you. I am giving you a copy of the song you sang with us on Christmas Eve. I'll always remember you. Love, Elfie."

"Granny, what did you tell him?" asked James.

"When Elfie and I were walking through the snowdrifts, I noticed he couldn't read any of the road signs until he was right on top of them. He couldn't see them because he needed glasses. Santa Claus went over to the work bench and found a pair of glasses that were just perfect for Elfie."

"Oh Granny! You really met Elfie and Santa Claus. Were you ever lucky!" beamed James.

"I'll never forget that night. While singing a holiday jingle, the elves let me help them pack Santa's sleigh, and the very next thing I remembered I was back at home."

"Just then Santa Claus appeared, 'Ho! Ho! Ho! What do we have here? Elfie, why are you crying? Who is this little girl? You know I don't allow visitors here at Santa Land.'

'Hello Santa. I'm Jessica. Please don't be angry with Elfie. I asked him to bring me here so I could help him.'

I motioned to Santa asking him to bend down and then I whispered something in his ear. 'Ho! Ho! Ho! Jessica, I think you are right. I should have figured that out long ago.'"

"One tiny elf saw Elfie and he called out to the others, 'Hey look who's finally back. Hey Elfie, did you lose your way again?' A group of elves surrounded Elfie and teased him about forgetting to put wheels on the toy trains and putting soldier heads on the bodies of teddy bears.

I couldn't stand to hear how mean these little elves were being to Elfie, and I yelled really loudly. 'Stop it! Stop it! Stop teasing Elfie! He is a very kind and sad little elf, and maybe if you realized that you wouldn't be so cruel.'"

"Together, Elfie and I trudged through snowdrift after snowdrift until we finally found a tiny village. It was in the middle of nowhere. Elves of all different colors were busy packing Santa's bag. They were scurrying here and there.

And then I saw the reindeer! They were so huge and there seemed to be something magical about them. It was almost as if they understood every single word that was said," Granny continued.

'Oh Elfie! What do you mean you used to be one of the best toy makers?'

'I can't do anything right. Everything I touch turns out to be a disaster! All the other elves laugh at me and tell me I'm a terrible toy maker.'

'Oh Elfie! Let me help you. I know exactly how you feel. Ever since we've moved here I have been so unhappy. I don't have any friends, and I bet Santa Claus won't even know where to find me on Christmas Eve.'

'Oh, yes he does. Santa Claus knows everything. And I'd love to be your friend if you would like!'

'Elfie, I would love to have you for my friend. Since we're friends and friends help each other, let me help you. If you take me to Santa's workshop, I'll help you make the toys, and you'll be the best toymaker once again."'

'"Hello there, little blue elf! Why are you crying, and what are you doing all alone out here on such a cold night?' I asked.

'Oh, you wouldn't understand. Nobody can help me. I'm hopeless,' said the elf.

'Hopeless! Why would you say that?'

'Santa sent me on an errand and I got myself lost! I don't know where I am!'

'You know Santa?! The **real** Santa Claus?'

'Of course I do. I'm Elfie, one of Santa's helpers. I make toys for children all around the world, and I used to be one of the best toy makers around.'

"Alright James, I'll continue. I climbed out of my window and very cautiously made my way to see this unusual, little blue elf. He was so tiny, no higher than my knee. He had pointy ears and a very red nose.

He was dressed in a blue fuzzy jacket with matching pants, and his face was **really** blue. This tiny elf was so upset, he didn't even realize I was sitting next to him." Granny looked out the window and continued her story.

"One night, I thought I heard a strange noise outside of my bedroom window. It sounded like a very tiny squeaking mouse. Quickly, I jumped out of my bed and ran to look out of my window. There in the snow bank, I saw a tiny blue elf crying."

"Oh Granny! What did you do? Was he really blue? Did he talk to you or did he run away?" asked Rosy.

"Be quiet, Rosy. Let Granny finish the story," snapped James, who sat perfectly still, hanging onto every word Granny spoke.

"A very long time ago when I was just a little girl, my father was stationed to work at the North Pole. I was very unhappy about moving away and leaving my friends behind.

When we arrived at the North Pole, I couldn't believe how high the snowdrifts were and how cold it was. But the worst part was that I didn't have anyone to play with. Many nights I cried myself to sleep. I wished I could go back home, but I knew that was impossible. Christmas was getting closer and I didn't think Santa Claus would know where to find me."

"Time for bed children. It is almost nine o'clock and I promised your parents you would both be in bed before they get home," Granny announced as she slowly lifted herself out of her rocking chair.

"Oh Granny! We're not that tired yet. It's too early," stretched Rosy as she quickly covered her mouth mimicking a bedtime yawn.

"Yeah, Granny! Tell us a bedtime story. Tell us about one of your adventures that happened long, long ago," pleaded James as he tugged on her fuzzy blue sweater.

"Well, children, I have one adventure that I've never shared with another soul. A very long time ago I made a promise to a very special friend of mine and I'm not sure you can keep a secret," said Granny with a twinkle in her eye.

"Yes, we can Granny. I know we can," begged Rosy.

"Let's go upstairs and perhaps I'll let you in on a very secretive adventure," Granny whispered as they all made their way upstairs and sat down by James's bed.

FOR MOM

"But there's a story behind everything. How a picture got on the wall. How a scar got on your face. Sometimes the stories are simple, and sometimes they are hard and heartbreaking. But behind all your stories is always your mother's story, because hers is where yours begin."

- Mitch Albom

Elfie the Elf

Written By: Cheryl DeVleeschouwer

Illustrated By: Christian J. Gaitan

UPSIDE DOWN TALES

Cinderella

Here is Cinderella's version of this famous story

Turn the book over and read the story from her sister's point of view

A Citadel Press Book
Published by Carol Publishing Group

First Carol Publishing Group Edition 1992

A Citadel Press Book
Published by Carol Publishing Group
Citadel Press is a registered trademark of Carol Communications, Inc.

Editorial Offices : 600 Madison Avenue, New York, NY 10022
Sales & Distribution Offices: 120 Enterprise Avenue, Secaucus, NJ 07094
In Canada: Canadian Manda Group, P.O. Box 920, Station U, Toronto, Ontario, M8Z 5P9, Canada

Queries regarding rights and permissions should be addressed to Carol Publishing Group, 600 Madison Avenue, New York, NY 10022

Manufactured in the United States of America
ISBN 0-8065-1298-9

10 9 8 7 6 5 4 3 2 1

Carol Publishing Group books are available at special discounts for bulk purchases, for sales promotions, fund raising, or educational purposes. Special editions can also be created to specifications. For details contact: Special Sales Department, Carol Publishing Group, 120 Enterprise Ave., Secaucus, NJ 07094

Library of Congress Cataloging-in-Publication Data

Shorto, Russell.
    Cinderella and Cinderella's stepsister / Russell Shorto; illustrated by T. Lewis.
        p.   cm.

        Summary: After reading the classic tale of Cinderella, the reader is invited to turn the book upside down and read an updated version told from the "evil" stepsister's vantage point.
            1. Toy and movable books--Specimens. [1. Fairy tales.
2. Folklore. 3. Toy and movable books.] I. Lewis, T. (Thomas), ill. II. Title. III. Title: Cinderella's stepsister.
PZ8.S344C1   1990
[398.2]--dc20   90-41900
                                                              CIP
                                                              AC

Once there was a girl who lived with her father in a beautiful cottage on the edge of the forest.

One day the father brought home a new wife, who had two daughters of her own. These girls had pretty faces but wicked hearts. They began ordering the man's daughter about like a servant.

The daughter worked day and night to please her stepsisters. Her nice clothes became rags. She was always covered with soot and cinders from cleaning the fireplace in the kitchen. The wicked stepsisters only made fun of her. "Look at her hair!" the older one said rudely. "It is full of cinders."

"So it is!" said the younger one. "Let's call her Cinderella!"

The two stepsisters laughed and laughed, and from that moment on they called the poor girl *Cinderella.*

One day word came that a great ball was to be held at the palace. The handsome prince would choose his bride at the ball. As Cinderella helped her stepsisters get ready, she asked, "What about me? Can't *I* come to the ball?"

The stepsisters could hardly believe their ears. "*You?*" they exclaimed. "You are so grubby and plain. Imagine the prince choosing you!" They laughed and laughed. Then they hopped into their carriage and were whisked off to the palace.

Cinderella watched the carriage disappear, tears streaming down her face. "I may be plain and grubby," she whispered, "but I would still like to go to the ball." She had forgotten that underneath the soot and cinders she was really a beautiful girl.

Suddenly a bright light appeared behind Cinderella. She turned around to find a strange woman with wings dressed in a long, silver cloak.

"I am your Fairy Godmother," the woman told Cinderella. "I have come to grant your wish. You are a good girl, and you deserve to go to the ball."

Cinderella dried her eyes. "But how can I?" she asked. "I have no coach. I have no horses. I have no fine gown."

"Tut tut!" the Fairy Godmother said, smiling. And, waving her magic wand, she turned a pumpkin into a beautiful gilded coach.

"Oh my! How wonderful!" cried Cinderella.

Then the Fairy Godmother spotted six mice scampering in the grass. With a wave of her wand they were changed into six horses.

Next she spied an old weasel sitting by the gate. She waved her wand again, and the weasel turned into a coachman—with the finest set of whiskers imaginable!

Then the Fairy Godmother turned to Cinderella
and waved her wand a final time. Cinderella's
tattered dress became a shimmering silver-blue ball
gown, and her old wooden shoes turned into slender
glass slippers.

"Oh, Fairy Godmother," Cinderella said softly,
"how can I thank you?"

"Never mind me," the Fairy Godmother replied. "You just hurry to the ball. But remember one thing: at midnight everything will become as it was. So, my dear, you must leave the ball before the last stroke of twelve!"

And with that, the coachman opened the door and bowed. Cinderella stepped into the coach and was swept off to the ball.

At the palace, everyone asked the same question: "Who is that beautiful girl with the glass slippers?" Even Cinderella's stepsisters did not recognize her.

The prince was enchanted by her beauty, and the amazing stories she told him about mice and pumpkins. He danced with her all evening, and Cinderella had a wonderful time.

Suddenly she heard the clock begin to chime twelve. "Oh I'm sorry, Your Majesty," Cinderella cried, "but I must go!" And she ran down the steps and out of the palace.

She reached the gates just in time to watch her coach turn back into a pumpkin. Her horses became scampering mice again, and the coachman slithered away as a weasel. She looked down and saw that her beautiful gown was once more only a ragged old dress.

The prince ran outside, but he saw only a tearful girl in a tattered dress hurrying down the road. Then he spotted something on the steps. It was a slender glass slipper. The prince picked it up and gave it to his footman. "Search the kingdom for the owner of this slipper!" he commanded. "She is to be my bride!"

The prince's men searched high and low. They went to every home and asked every young lady to try on the slipper. But the slipper was too small for all of them.

Finally the men came to Cinderella's house. The elder stepsister eagerly took the slipper. Try as she might, she could not get her foot into it. "Ouch!"

she finally cried. The younger stepsister snatched the slipper to try her luck. But it didn't fit her any better.

"Are there any other women in the house?" the prince's footman asked.

"There is only our grubby stepsister, Cinderella," answered the elder sister.

"Bring her here!" commanded the footman.

So Cinderella was called in from the kitchen, where she was busy scrubbing the floor. She sat down shyly, and stretched out her slender foot. The prince himself knelt and put the slipper on her foot.

Everyone gasped. *A perfect fit!*

The prince gazed into the girl's face and saw that she was indeed his true love. "My dear!" he cried.

"But I am only a poor, ragged girl with cinders in her hair," said Cinderella sadly.

"Nonsense!" the prince declared. "You are my beloved. We shall be married on Saturday."

And so poor Cinderella became the princess of the kingdom, and nobody was so surprised as her stepsisters at the way things turned out.

Cinderella and the prince lived happily ever after, and that's the end of the story.

Or is it? Turn the book over . . . and we shall see!